PAROMITA

PAROMITA

Sumathi Sudhakar

Rupa & Co

Published 2002 by
Rupa . Co
7/16, Ansari Road, Daryaganj,
New Delhi 110 002

Sales Centres:

Allahabad Bangalore Chandigarh Chennai
Dehradun Hyderabad Jaipur Kathmandu
Kolkata Ludhiana Mumbai Pune

Commissioning Editor: Paro Anand
Illustrations: Moonis Ijlal

ISBN 81-7167-979-X

Typeset 12 pts. Aldine by
Nikita Overseas Pvt Ltd,
1410 Chiranjiv Tower,
43 Nehru Place
New Delhi 110 019

Printed in India by
Saurabh Print-O-Pack,
A-15-16, Sector-IV, Noida 201 301

I dedicate this novel to my wonderful parents, who have always been my inspiration and my strength

CONTENTS

PAROMITA:
A CURTAIN RAISER

I t was a momentous campaign. Millions of young Indian girls would have joined in the movement with fervour for it directly affected their present and their future. Only not many of them knew that it was happening. They were on blinkers that restricted their vision, and reins that were firmly grasped by a heartless society.

And then came some enlightened men: Raja Ram Mohan Roy, Pandit Ishwarchandra Vidyasagar and Keshub Chandra Sen in Bengal, among others. They slowly but surely built up that campaign that we began talking about.

This campaign that began in the 1800s tried to restore to girls some basic rights that they had lost, such as the right to education. It also tried to free them from evil practices that had made their lives miserable: practices such as sati, child marriage and exploitation of young widows.

If you were a girl of nine or ten in India in the early 1800s, like the heroine of our story, Paromita is—you can bet on it—you wouldn't be in school. O no! Your parents would have been actively seeking the right 'boy' for you! And believe this or not, the 'boy' chosen for you might even be fifty years of age or more!

In the eighteenth and early nineteenth century, the status of women in Indian society was very sorry indeed. Girls were not sent to school, they were married at a very young age, and often, to much older men.

When these old husbands died, the young widows spent a miserable life in seclusion. They were considered inauspicious and not allowed to participate in festivities. In some parts of the country, they were forced to shave their heads. They could neither wear bright dresses, nor adorn themselves with jewels and flowers. They were expected to fast and worship and pray all the time. They ate only sparsely, met few people and generally, lived a very drab and severe life.

In some communities, the young widow would be forced to enter the funeral pyre of her husband and give up her life. This practice was called sati. A woman who joined her husband in death was a true, loyal wife, said the orthodox members of the society. This was more so, when the dead men had left behind a lot of wealth. Greedy relatives would force his widow to become a sati so that they could take over his wealth and property.

There was little that the parents of the girls could do. Often they were so poor and so afraid of the society they lived in, that they could not stand up to it and question its practices. If they resisted the injustice being done to their daughters, society might condemn them or even ostracize them. And then what would happen to their other children? Remember, in those days, families were big.

Sometimes, when people had female babies, they killed them at birth. This was called female infanticide. Who knows why this happened? Perhaps the thought of the miserable life that was in store for young girls was too unbearable for the parents. Perhaps they wanted to spare their babies this torture. Perhaps they simply could not afford the marriage and other expenses that would follow, when a female baby was born. Whatever the reason, you will agree, that this was wrong. It was evil: to kill an innocent baby for no fault other than that it was a girl.

Raja Ram Mohan Roy, one of the earliest social reformers of Bengal, was horrified to see a young widow in his family forced to become a sati. He walked out of his family in disgust and began travelling and reading widely. He studied both Indian and western literature and philosophy. He wanted his countrymen to be educated. He said that they should open their eyes to what was happening around them in the world.

He declared that Hindu religion did not demand the sati of a widow and he actively campaigned against the practice. Naturally the orthodox society did not like this. But he put so much pressure on the English administration, that they introduced the Prohibition of Suttee Act in 1829. He was well supported by the growing numbers of educated and open-minded class of Indians.

The other great reformer of the 1800s was Ishwarchandra Vidyasagar. He was a brilliant Sanskrit scholar and an educationist. He was an active campaigner for women's rights. He was responsible for getting the age of marriage of girls fixed at a much higher age than it was.

He felt that it was wrong to penalize young widows for the death of their husbands: why should they lead a life of penance and austerity when they were still children? He believed that widows should be remarried. Pandit Vidyasagar conducted many widow remarriages. He even got his own son married to a young widow.

Now this may not appear as a great feat to you. But do keep in mind the society that he lived in. This society was dominated by an orthodox class of people, who disapproved of his activity.

Vidyasagar was an extraordinary man. Being a Sanskrit scholar, he used the scriptures to show to this society that their religion did not actually advocate such ill treatment of women. Somewhere down the centuries, some people had misinterpreted the scriptures and women had lost their rights.

Vidyasagar managed to influence the English administration to introduce the Widow Remarriage Act, which was passed in 1858.

He also insisted that girls should be educated and encouraged to make decisions in their lives. He set up many model schools for girls.

Our story, *Paromita*, shows the influence of Vidyasagar on the rural society of Bengal. The story is set in the early 1850s. Although the Prohibition of Suttee Act had been passed in 1829, the evil practice would not have died out immediately. In *Paromita,* you hear of a girl who had become a sati. You can feel the influence of that terrible happening and the magnetic attraction of the girls' school on young Paromita, the nine-year old heroine of the story.

The early nineteenth century was actually a watershed in the history of Indian society. There was a radical change in the thinking of the people. The reforms that were introduced in this period had a tremendous impact on the generations that followed.

If every town and village has a school and millions of students attend these schools today, it is largely because of the passionate commitment of people like Ram Mohan Roy, Vidyasagar and several others. If you look forward confidentiy to a bright future today, you have to thank these far-thinking pioneers for it.

Girls have been girls all along. Their impulses and feelings, liked and dislikes, and desires could not have been too different then from what they are now. Only circumstances were different. In our heroine Paromita, you will see a young and energetic spirit struggling to shrug off its shackles and soar into the open skies.

Look deep within yourself: do you see a Paromita in you?

1

PARO'S DESIRE

She was young and she was charming. When little Paromita was happy, her laughter sounded like the gurgling of a river. Two deep dimples appeared on her soft pink cheeks and her dancing eyes danced more than ever. When she ran down the paddy fields of Gobindopur in Bengal, her long black hair and the *aanchal* of her plain sari streaming behind her, even the cuckoos stopped their sweet cooing to watch the sight.

She was popular with all the children of the village, and with most of the adults too.

Paromita was all of nine years, and she lived in the small village of Gobindopur with her parents and her brother Debanshu. She spent her days skipping down the paddy fields and the forests fringing the village, splashing in the cool waters of the pools and plucking a wide variety of fruits from the trees that grew everywhere. There were *chikus* that tasted like sugar candy, and mangoes, bananas and melons. There were berries: some small and round and purple, that stained her mouth a lovely deep violet, and others juicy, white and pink, that filled her mouth with sweet juice when she sank her pearl white teeth into them.

She was a born leader and on days when she felt quite, quite chirpy—which was most of the time—she led her gang of little boys and girls on a rowdy cattle hunt! They would start out in the morning and chase the herds of cows that were being taken for grazing by cowherd boys not much older than them! The gang would boo and scream and chase the cows, which would run pell-mell, much to the chagrin of the cowherds who would flail their sticks in an attempt to round up the cows again!

Her mother, Mrinalini Devi, would then have to listen to the comments and complaints of some of the elderly village women who disapproved of Paro's sprightly ways. "You should keep her indoors!" one old woman had advised. "She is too old to be playing with the boys."

"Why don't you get her married? If you let her expose herself like this she will earn a bad name for herself and for you," said Chitra *boudi,* her neighbour.

Paro's mother sighed. "Surely Sri Krishna's mother Jashoda must have felt like this when the women of Brindaban complained to her about Krishna's pranks!" she thought. "If only Paro was a boy like Krishna! I really would not have to worry much about her! I wonder what Jashoda would have done if Krishna had been a girl!"

And then one day, Paro's father caught her in the act! Paro, with a small straw basket in her hand, was plucking hibiscus flowers from the large bush in Chitra *boudi's* garden. Chitra *boudi,* standing on her threshold, saw a pair of small hands nimbly bend the slender stalk of the hibiscus and neatly pluck flowers, one after another. "Caught you, *dooshtu* Paro!" she thought as she silently crept up to the unsuspecting girl who was behind the bush and could not see her.

When Paro's hand came up to pluck another flower, Chitra *boudi* caught her by the wrist. "So you're the thief who has been stripping my bush of its flowers! Now what shall I do with you, you *badmash?*"

"*O mashi,* surely you don't mind me plucking some *jaba phool* for the *thakur's puja?*" she said, and her laughing eyes confronted Chitra *boudi's,* teasing, provoking and challenging her to turn down this perfectly logical request.

But Chitra was not one to be put down by a mere girl. She tucked in the *aanchal* of her *sari* tightly at her waist and answered back, "I need the flowers for worshipping the *thakur* in *my* house!" But this did not deter Paro. Pat came her rejoinder. Her round eyes opened wide and looked ever so innocent as she said, "But *thakur* is *thakur* everywhere, isn't it, *mashi*? So what difference does it make whether you use the flowers or I use them for worship?" Chitra gasped in surprise. She did not expect such a reply from this chit of a girl!

Paro wrenched her wrist away and dashed off, her laughter tinkling behind her. She ran straight into her father who was at their doorstep and had watched the entire proceedings. "Watch where you're going," he said as she rammed into him. "And you had better not run around the village like a rowdy boy. You're a growing girl, remember? Sit at home and help your mother!" *"Accha, baba!"* she replied, casting her eyes down and slipping into the kitchen.

'I must begin to think about her marriage before she runs wild and uncontrollable!' thought her father as he left the house.

Although Mrinalini engaged her young daughter in small chores around the house, she knew she could never rein Paro's spirit. Paro would quickly complete whatever odd jobs her mother gave her and speed away to join her friends out in the fields.

Only one thing could stop Paro in her tracks: the sight of school children walking down to the school, with their books, slates and chalk pieces. She loved to watch them rush to school and she loved to listen to them recite poems and lessons in their classroom. She would often stand motionless outside the school, listening to the teacher teach them to write and count, and tell them all about the wide world. It made her want to study too.

In fact, this was the biggest regret of her young life: that she was not sent to school, while her elder brother Debu was. She saw him packed off to school every day with his big bags winging from his shoulder. But his school did not admit girls.

The closest girls' school was in Sonapara village across river Damodar.

She had been excited when the girls' school was inaugurated four months ago. Ishwarchandra Vidyasagar *moshai* himself had come from Kolkata for the inauguration. So many uncles from Gobindopur had gone for the function. They had all vowed to send their daughters to the school. But after Vidyasagar *moshai* left Sonapara, life had returned to normal and all the promises had been forgotten. Today, only a few girls from Gobindopur were ferried across the river everyday to attend school at Sonapara.

Among them were Sucharita, Charulata and Ruma. Earlier they had been part of Paro's gang. In fact Sucharita was quite an expert at bringing down mangoes from trees by stoning them. This skill had made her a key member of Paro's gang. But now none of them could find the time for anything more than a brief game now and then. What with school and lessons to be learnt, and with helping mother at home, their hands were full.

But Paro did not resent the fact that the girls' school had snatched her friends away from her. She only wished that she could join them too. Every morning as they were escorted to the river bank to catch the ferry, Paro's eager eyes would follow them till they were out of sight. She would wistfully watch their quick, eager steps, their books and bags and their excited chatter. What new thing would they learn today, she wondered? If only she could go to school…!

"*Baba,* send me to school too!" she pleaded one day when her father, Hariprasad Choudhry, was just leaving home for the fields.

Hariprasad was a small landlord and they were going through difficult times. Bengal was just recovering from a famine that had crippled two generations of small farmers like him. The famine had happened more than eighty years ago, but it had left its scar on two or more generations of small landlords. It was only now that he had completely come out of the effect of the famine!

And to top it all, the English rulers…the less said about them the better. He had to pay a fat sum as revenue to the administration and it did not matter if his harvest was poor. And who dared raise their voice against the white men?

Ok, in the city some men did raise their voices…but here in the villages, these men were mere names…

Images of his father's struggle flitted across Hariprasad's mind. His father had often recounted the stories of his grim beginnings… the poverty, the starvation, the agony of watching your brothers and sisters die for want of food and water helplessly! The words still rang in his mind and stabbed at his soul.

How could he make Paro understand that educating a girl was a big struggle that he did not have the courage to undertake. He had grown up, a tired son of a tired father, for whom the struggle of existence had been all that they could undertake. The terrible famine of the 1760s had claimed so many lives. Grandfather had defied all odds to keep his body and soul together and feed the seven children that survived, out of the eleven that had been born to him.

In his time, father had, through his efforts and because of better rains and harvests, purchased a little land and saw his sons reasonably educated. He had got his three daughters married into comfortable families. But that was all. He left property of very little value for his sons.

Hariprasad's struggle had begun early in life. He had worked hard to consolidate his earnings and make his family comfortable. It was only now that his family had been accepted and acknowledged by the society of well to do farmers in the neighbourhood.

It would never do to irk this society's wrath by educating a girl. The society did not approve of such things. Girls should be married young and live a demure life of service. Of what use was education to them? Hariprasad knew that it would serve nobody's purpose if he sent Paro to school.

But little Paro wouldn't understand all that. He turned to her with a smile: "Why do you want to trouble yourself so much, *mamoney?* My pretty *shonamoney* will soon be a bride and live grandly in a *raja's* palace!"

Paro blushed and skipped away. Marriage! She thought and imagined herself as the bride—with *alta* on her feet and dots of *chandan* on her brows, red *sindoor* in the parting of her hair, a sari of red and gold, beautiful *shankha* and *pola* bangles adorning her slender wrists, and ever so many jewels. Lovely sweets and *payesh* and so many wonderful dishes to eat—there was nothing quite like a wedding feast! And everyone would pet her and say she looked beautiful! And as for the *baur!* Paro stopped, frowning. Why could she not imagine the *baur,* the groom she would marry?

She forgot it all in a trice as she saw Ruma beckon her from far. It was a week since she had chatted with the school-going Ruma. What fun! Paro skipped away, marriage forgotten!

Later when her brother sat working out sums on the slate in the evening, she sat beside him and asked him endless questions. Debu, with his perpetually tousled hair and round eyes, was a quiet and studious boy of twelve. Besides the round eyes, there was little resemblance between brother and sister. She was a free spirit; he was inhibited and introverted. He could rarely express himself openly on anything, and when he did, he was easily put down.

Debu loved and admired his kid sister's charming openness and independence and secretly wished that he could be like her too. He swelled with pride when she came to him for lessons everyday: this brave and beautiful sister of his actually sought him out for lessons! He patiently taught her to read and write, and sing out poems. She could multiply with speed and was quick at understanding mathematics.

2

PARO'S MARRIAGE

hen one day, her father announced that Paro was
to be married soon. The would-be bridegroom was
Manik *babu*, the big *zamindar* of the village. He had
a big bungalow and lots of money and two horse carriages
and ever so many *bigha* of agricultural lands. Manik *babu's*
gold chains glittered and winked in the sun when he rode
through the village on his horse carriage. So Paro's father
was happy for her. But Paro was not happy; nor was Debu;
and their quiet mother who always seemed to have melted
into the background, was not happy either.

They were not happy because Manik *babu* was nearly
seventy-five years of age. Poor child, to be married to a man
old enough to be her grandfather or maybe a great
grandfather!

As soon as father announced it, there was silence in the house. The first to react was Debu, who shouted hysterically: "*Na, na na!* That old man may die any day and what will happen to poor Paro? Do you want to make her a *sati* like Nandana!"

Thrrrr...ash

The slap his father gave sent Debu crashing against the wall. His mother shut her eyes and wept. She had never opened her mouth against her husband. Even the thought of her young daughter married to an old man and the sight of her growing son being slapped by his father could not wring out a word of protest from her. She had never learnt to speak out.

Debu's words caused a crease to appear on Paro's brow. She had never seen her quiet brother shout. And never, indeed, had he opposed their father. He had taken a painful beating for supporting her. Surely there was something in what he had said. Paro turned to stone.

Nandana! The name brought back memories, some sweet, some sad and some quite heartbreaking. Memories of a wedding feast and lots of fun and games... followed by a tearful farewell, parting from one's parents and playmates and going away to a distance village...!

Paro remembered that when Nandana had got married, she had wondered why she was marrying such an old man. He had white hair and he had caused quite a sensation in the marriage *pandal* when one of his *paan*-stained teeth fell out during the ceremony! How all the girls had giggled and how their parents had frowned at them so fiercely that they straightened their faces with an effort.

Paro had tried to imagine Nandana living among strangers in a strange new place, cooking for her husband, bringing pots of water, cleaning, scrubbing, washing, praying and doing the hundred and one never-ending chores that she saw her mother do everyday.

Would Nandana often think of *her* mother? Who in her new house would take just one look at her face and understand how she felt or what she wanted, as only her mother could?

Nandana had been thirteen when she was married and sent away. Paro had heard some elderly women whisper at the wedding that Nandana should have been married three years back. She had outgrown the age of marriage!

Then came that letter some months later that brought the dreadful news...the news of Nandana's death. The entire village had been shattered by the piercing screams of Nandana's poor mother and the bewildered and frightened wails of her younger sister, Sarbari.

The story was told in hushed whispers. Nandana's husband had died of some dreadful disease. And when he was cremated, Nandana had been big-hearted enough to join her husband on the funeral pyre. She had not wanted to live after her husband's death. She had become Ma *Sati*. She would be a shining example to generations of young women in the village.

But her mother had been inconsolable for days. Her father had been bitter and angry. He had ranted and raved and talked about lodging a police complaint, until the scandalized village convinced him against doing this and shushed the whole matter up. True, Nandana's parents should have been informed of their son-in-law's death. They should have been told of Nandana's decision before the terrible event. How could a daughter become a *sati* without the knowledge of the parents? The village in its wisdom sympathised with the parents of the unfortunate girl.

But...the wise men said, becoming a *sati* was an important social custom and hence, must be accepted stoically. What a noble soul their daughter had been. How wise for her age!

And then someone came from the village where Nandana had lived. They spoke of the young girl being dragged through the streets screaming with terror, and being thrust into the funeral pyre. The villagers pretended not to have heard any of it. Only Nandana's parents, her sister and her playmates had cried and cried on hearing of it.

Paro's thoughts jerked back to the present. *Dada* was right. What if her old *baur* too died very soon...would she have to become a *sati*? But she wanted to live long, to play and have fun, to go to school and study, write on the slate and read books, wear spectacles and look wise and when

she grew up, teach other little girls like her! She did not want to be cast into the fire... how hot the flames must be!

All her dreams would turn to ashes with her. How could her father dream of marrying her off to that old Manik *babu*? He was so old; he had to peer through his glasses to see anything. She had seen him many times, getting in or out of his horse–drawn carriage. Two servants would pop from nowhere, one with an umbrella to hold over his bald head, and another with a pair of shoes, that he would kneel and fit into the old man's feet.

Would she have to do that if she were married
   to him? Ugh!
Surely he would dash all her dreams by dying
   soon!
No! She could not let that happen!
She **would** not let that happen!

That day the spring went out of Paro's steps, her eyes lost their twinkle and the dimples stopped appearing on her tender cheeks. "I won't become a *sati* like Nandana," she vowed to herself, as she picked up a pot and started for *thakurpukur*, the big pond next to the *Kalibari*, the temple of Mother Kali.

3

PARO MEETS MASTERMOSHAI

At the edge of Gobindopur, fringing the forest was the *Kalibari*. It was an old, old temple of Kali, the fierce and powerful form of the mother goddess. The black stone idol was quite frightening, with its angry eyes and the red tongue hanging out of the mouth.

More frightening than even the goddess was the old, bent *purohit* who looked after the temple and conducted the rituals there. He lived in a little hut overlooking the lovely pond, *thakurpukur,* which was dedicated to the temple. He never smiled and always shooed away the children, who frequented *thakurpukur,* drawn by its cool waters.

It was said that he opened the temple to a gang of dacoits at night, who would come in from the forest and offer animal sacrifices to the goddess. Nobody had quite seen any of it, and nobody talked openly. But the story floated around in the breeze and everyone knew it!

Today, as she passed *Kalibari*, Paro did not see *purohit*. He must have gone into the forest for firewood, fruits and flowers as he often did.

Paro stopped and put down her pot. As usual, she closed her eyes and folded her hands in a namoshkar, mumbling the little prayer that her mother had taught her. But she was not done with the goddess yet. She had come with a petition and she uttered it loud and clear, so that the goddess might not miss even the least of her words!

"*Ma*, give me strength. Take care of me. Make me a strong girl," said Paro. "I don't want to get married. I want to study and grow into a wise girl and teach other girls at the village school. But I don't want to get married - *not now*, at least. *Ma*, bless me so that my wishes might come true."

As she spoke aloud to the mother goddess, she did not notice that she was being watched.

Biswajit, the teacher at the girls' school at Sonapara, who had come to visit his grandmother at Gobindopur, watched the girl quietly. He was short and stocky, and he had soulful eyes behind round spectacles, which gave him a very intellectual look. He was amused to see the solemn face of the girl.

"I'm sure *ma* will bless you," he said, going up to her. But Paro just looked up at him, startled, and then picking up her pot, ran away.

"*Ma go,* who could he be?" she wondered, half in fear, as she dipped her pot into the pond.

Sarbari was at the pond too. She was Nandana's sister and she went to school at Sonapara. After Nandana's death, there was a sea change in her family's approach to all matters. Her parents, who had once been very pious, now stopped visiting *Kalibari*. The villagers said they were very angry with the goddess for not having taken care of their dear daughter.

Then her father had put Sarbari to school. "She will go to school and then to college and become a doctor in the city!" he had sworn in public. The entire village had shut its ears when it heard this terrible oath. "*Durga, Durga!* Was this the way to bring up one's daughter?"

Sarbari was a meek girl and found it a little difficult to cope with her father's ambitions and society's open disapproval. But she was an obedient and bright child, and like the other school going girls of the village, she enjoyed going to school.

Sarbari and Paro were great friends. Before Nandana's death, Sarbari too had been part of Paro's gang, although a passive and quiet one, a follower rather than a leader. But she admired Paro's dynamism and Paro had always felt protective towards this mild girl. And there had developed a strange but strong bond between them.

As the two girls returned from the pond, the man was still in front of *Kalibari*.

"Who's he?" Paro asked in a whisper.

Sarbari answered: "He is the *mastermoshai* at our school."

Paro stood electrified. She put down the pot.

"Paro, what…?" but before Sarbari could complete her sentence, Paro had vanished from her side.

She was standing before the man, and looking at him steadily, she said, "*Mastermoshai,* will you take me to school?"

Biswajit was surprised too. This was no ordinary girl, he thought. There was fire in those big eyes.

"Of course," he replied. "But first, tell me who you are?"

"I am Paromita," she replied, looking him in the eye.

"And you are Sarbari's friend?" he asked, casting a friendly glance at Sarbari, who was hanging back and looking on.

"Yes, *mastermoshai*. She has told me all about her school and lessons. I too want to study!" Paro had not blinked even once so far.

"Of course!" replied Biswajit. "Come, let us go and tell your father that."

"*Na, na*" Paro was almost in a panic. It was as if a trance was broken. Her eyes darted here and there in utter confusion. "He would never agree. Don't tell him about it. But, but… please allow me to come to school every day!"

"But how can you come to school every day without your father's permission"? asked Biswajit.

"I…I'll…I'll somehow manage," said the girl, pleading with her eyes.

"No," said Biswajit kindly. "Let us talk to your father and convince him that girls must attend school…"

"*Baba* won't listen! He sends *dada* to school…but he won't send me. He says girls must not go to school."

"I'll convince him. Take me to your house. Let us not do anything without his permission. That is not a good idea!"

"It's no use!" said Paro, looking disappointed. Her eyes downcast and her shoulders drooping, she walked away to join Sarbari. Biswajit looked on, disturbed. The two friends walked back to their houses silently. As they parted, Sarbari said, "Don't worry, Paro. You'll get married soon and will forget about school…"

Lightning flashed from those eyes as Paro retorted, "I won't get married soon," and she marched off, chin in air…

4

WHERE IS PARO?

But soon Paro's wedding day drew near. The house began to look festive. Relatives walked in and out. The *moyra* and his men were making sweets in the great *pandal* in the backyard, just outside the kitchen. The clatter of big vessels, the sweet smoke of frying, and the collective aroma of many special dishes being cooked simultaneously added to the festive atmosphere. Only Paro looked most unhappy.

Two days before her wedding, she was stone-faced and sullen. Even the sight of her red and gold wedding sari did not bring a smile to her face. Her *thakurma* and *mejo pishi* were to arrive that day. The other two *pishis* were expected to arrive the next day.

After lunch, her mother smeared *alta* on her tender feet, but Paro who loved *alta*, would not react at all. Debu, who was looking on, got this strange feeling that she was up to something. Paro went to sit out in the front yard, while the *alta* dried.

That evening Swarnalata, the children's favourite *mejo pishi,* arrived from Nabadwip. She called for Paro loudly as she entered the house.

"Aashun, aashun, mejdi!" Mrinalini welcomed her sister-in-law with affection. "Why, didn't you see Paro outside in the yard? She was sitting there just some time ago!"

"Koi, na to!" answered Swarnalata, who had come laden with a box full of her best saris and jewels—all for her favourite niece's wedding.

"She must have gone to Sarbari's house," put in Debu, who was tying some festoons in the house. But he spoke without conviction.

"But I told her not to go anywhere!" his mother was quite upset. "A bride in two days and she goes roaming out today! Will she never understand? Her father will be terribly angry if he hears of it. And what will *sasuima* say when she arrives to find the bride missing from the house?" Mrinalini was quite agitated. Her husband had gone to fetch his mother from his brother's house from a nearby village. And they were expected any moment.

"Baccha meye to!" said *Swarnalata,* with sympathy. "Do call her, *boudi.* I think she'll like this wedding gift I've

brought for her! Look *boudi!* How do you like this?" Like a magician performing a trick, she fished into one of her bags and pulled out a box. She pulled out the wedding gift. "I want to see if these bangles fit her little hand," she said, displaying a pair of gleaming gold bangles.

"Ba! ki sundar!" Paro's mother exclaimed as she examined the bangles. Her tired and tense face broke into a smile of pleasure. "Surely this will bring the cheer back to Paro's face!" she thought. She had been so worried by her daughter's grim appearance since the marriage had been announced. "Debu, *shona,* please bring Paro back from Sarbari's house!"

Debu dropped the festoons that he was tying and sped away.

But Paro was not at Sarbari's house. "She did not come here at all," said Sarbari's mother to Debu. He was surprised.

…At home, *thakurma* arrived, calling for her *shonamoney.* Mrinalini trembled, wondering what to say. But *thakurma* suddenly noticed her daughter from Nabadwip. She swept across the room and gathered her in her arms. *"Amar lokkhi meyeti!* How long is it since I saw you? When did you come?"

Debu hurried to all her friends' houses, but she was nowhere. "I haven't seen her today," said Sucharita.

"I don't know! I just got back from my *dadu's* house," said Ruma.

"Paro *di*?! No, she is not here. She has not been playing with us for some time now," said young Jago, one of Paro's old gang.

"Why? What's happened? Isn't she to be married tomorrow?" asked Jago's mother, coming to the threshold on hearing their voices. Debu was puzzled. Where could he look next?

Meanwhile Chitra *boudi* had appeared at the doorstep of Paro's house. "Swarna! *Mashi* ma!" she exclaimed and draping her *aanchal* over her head, she touched the old lady's feet reverentially. There was a gush of conversation and Paro's father walked out of the room, looking important and satisfied. Mrinalini sighed in relief and prayed that her children might return soon. Then no one need know that Paro had been missing.

Debu ran past the paddy fields and the banana groves. Now he was quite frantic. He peeped into *Kalibari* and ran to *thakurpukur*, but there was no sign of Paro anywhere.

...The excitement subsided and everybody suddenly remembered the bride. "Where is she? The bride?" exclaimed Chitra *boudi*, the nosiest of the lot, looking all around the room and peering into the inner rooms. Mrinalini, who had been dreading just this moment, stammered, "She...she...she will be here... soon."

...Her voice trailed off as Debu appeared at the door. Alone. "*Ma*," he burst out, half in terror and half in worry. "Paro is nowhere!"

This caused a sensation. Paro's father burst into the crowded room.

"What do you mean?" he demanded in a harsh voice.

"...I looked everywhere. Paro is not in the village. Nobody has seen her since this afternoon."

There was panic, anger and hysteria. Mrinalini reeled and clutched the wall for support. Swarnalata screamed and burst into tears. *Thakuma* was shocked. "Ki *kando! Sarbonash!*" she cried loudly. Chitra *boudi* began consoling everyone.

But in her heart of hearts, she was quite thrilled with all the excitement, and vaguely happy too, to find her old enemy in trouble. "That Paro!" she thought with malicious satisfaction. "I always knew she would do something like this!"

"Find that irresponsible girl immediately!" Debu's father's voice sounded like a whiplash. A big search was launched.

5

DILEMMA

Debu was confused. He did not know whether to be happy or upset: happy, because Paro had escaped that hateful marriage, and upset because who knew where his darling sister was and what trouble she was facing. As he thought more and more about it, he began to worry. Was she safe? Could she be in danger? Did she need help? Would they see her again? What would happen if she was caught and brought back? And again, what would she do all alone in the big world, a little girl with nobody to help her and take care of her?

These and many more questions whirred past one another in his mind, and caused deep furrows to appear on his young forehead. "Where has Paro gone?" wailed his mother and this jolted Debu out of his thoughts.

Indeed, nobody seemed to have seen the girl since that afternoon.

He walked out of the house, frowning. Where had Paro disappeared?

...Only one person seemed to have a clue. A niggling doubt had crept into young Sarbari's mind as she watched the entire village hunting for her friend.

"Could she have gone to my school at Sonapara?" she wondered.

She knew how badly Paro had wanted to go to school. May be she had run away to school as an escape from marriage. Should she tell anyone about her doubt? If she were right, Paro would be found at the school, brought back and married off to that old man! Would she face the same fate as her sister, Nandana? Sarbari's eyes filled with tears.

Nine-year-old Sarbari's memories of her dead sister were few: some games that they had played together, the sister dressed as a beautiful bride, leaving their home with a tearful face...and then that letter. They had not seen Nandana since her marriage. That *bidai* had become her final farewell! Would the same happen to Paro? How could she let that happen? *"Jak..besh holo!"* thought Sarbari. Paro would be happier away from Gobindopur.

But then...how could she keep quiet and let Paro's family down? How upset her mother must be! How worried her father must be! They would not even dream of searching at Sonapara.

It was Sunday tomorrow and there would be no school. How could she find out if she was right? Had Paro found her way or had she lost her way? Was she in some trouble?

What if Paro was in danger? If she had lost her way? What would she eat? Where would she sleep that night?... And what would she do if the *dakats,* who came to the temple every night, found her...would they make a *bali* of her to the goddess? Sarbari shivered in fear.

And there were wild animals in the forest that sometimes came out into the villages and roads....jackals and leopards that the villagers had seen. Maybe even a tiger, who knows?

Poor Sarbari. She did not quite know what to do. She who had been shielded and supported by Paro in all their games now felt responsible and anxious for her leader's safety. The protected wanted to become the protector!

Sarbari was in a dilemma. It was getting dark and the search had been intensified. But Paro was not found.

At last, she decided to pour out her doubts and fears to Debu*da*. He was big. He would know what to do next. She slipped out of her house and went looking for him.

She found Debu sitting on the banks of *thakurpukur,* weeping. "Debu*da,* I think I know where Paro has gone," announced young Sarbari.

6

PARO ON HER WAY

Sarbari was right, of course. Paro was on her way to Sonapara to meet *mastermoshai*. When she sneaked out of the house on Saturday afternoon, no one had quite noticed her. Everyone was too busy with the preparations for her marriage.

Paro ran past *Kalibari*, past Debu's school, along the banana groves, and through the paddy fields till she reached the bank of river Damodar. The river sprawled in front of her and she could hardly see the other bank from where she hid. And yet she knew it was not so difficult to cross the river, for did Sarbari and Sucharita and Ruma not go everyday to school across the Damodar?

Though there were regular ferries across the river to Sonapara, which took the girls to the school everyday, she knew she could not hope to take a boat. She had no money!

Besides the boatmen knew her too well: they had often been the butt of her pranks. While they sat gossiping in their boats anchored to the bank, she and her friends would creep up behind them and throw stones into the water just in front of them. The water would splash into their surprised faces and they would turn around gasping and spluttering. *"Badmaish meye!"* they would yell, shaking their fists at the fast disappearing backs of Paro and her gang.

Would the boatmen help her today?

She was gasping and panting as she contemplated the river from behind a bush. Her long hair was dishevelled and her sari had been frayed where it had been caught in some thorny bushes on the way. Her tender ankles had been pricked by thorns too, and beads of ruby-red blood peeped out of her fair ankles. But who cared? She had set a target for herself and Paro was not one to be discouraged by thorny ways!

Then she remembered the narrow bridge across the river some distance away where it became a mere stream. She had heard some villagers say that they walked across that bridge although it meant a tiresome walk. Little Paro did not stop to think that it might be a long way off.

She trudged along the course of the river in the direction of the bridge. An hour later, she came to it. By this time, she was so tired and hungry that she could hardly

walk. Dusk was falling and it would soon be dark. Like all young children, Paro too was afraid of the dark. She was anxious to reach the school before night fell.

The wooden bridge was narrow and it hung precariously across the river. As it was growing dark, there was no one walking across it and the young girl, her heart thudding with fear, set her foot on it. It was a good hour when she got off the bridge.

She instinctively moved along the mud road that led winding into the quickly gathering dark. When she saw some women scuttling along in front of her, she called out, *"Mashi ma! O mashi ma!"* The women turned around. She ran to join them. "I want to go to Sonapara! How far is it from here?" she asked, gasping for breath.

7

SENSATION IN GOBINDOPUR

At Gobindopur, Debu jumped up on hearing what Sarbari said. "What do you mean? Where is she?" he asked, wiping his tears on his *panjabi*. Then Sarbari, stammering and stumbling over her words, explained to him all her fears and doubts. How Paro had often talked of school and how she had met *mastermoshai* at this very *Kalibari* one day and had begged him to admit her to school without her father's knowledge. Out tumbled the whole story, in incoherent bits and pieces.

When she finished, Debu was convinced. "You're right!" he said quietly. "Yes, she always wanted to go to school. Why didn't I think of it?"

And then a thought struck him and he looked at the girl's young face, trembling with fear and panic: "My god! Could Paro be crossing the river now—in this dark? Why, some crocodile might kill her? She might drown! She does not know the way. We have wasted too much time! Sarbari, you fool! Why didn't you tell me this earlier when I came to your house? Why, why?"

He took the girl by her frail shoulders and shook her till her teeth chattered and she burst out crying. "Debu*da*, stop! Stop! I didn't think of it earlier. I'm sorry!" Slowly, the boy calmed down. "Go to my house and tell my parents that I've gone looking for Paromita and will be back with her. Don't tell them that I'm going to the girls' school at Sonapara because we're not sure yet that she is there."

He turned, and in a trice he was gone. It was growing dark now and Sarbari was terribly worried for him and Paro. But she dutifully carried the message back to Debu's house.

Poor Sarbari. She reached Debu's house at just the wrong moment.

Just ten minutes before she entered the house, Debu's parents had had a most unwelcome guest.

This was the personal assistant of Manik *babu*, Paro's bridegroom. And he had brought with him a shameful message. "We have heard rumours that your daughter Paromita has run away from home. My master wants to know if that is true." Paro's father had not known what to say.

"She is a playful child. She must be hiding somewhere. We're looking for her. She should be here anytime now," he blabbered.

But the fierce looking assistant was not impressed. "My master said that if your daughter does not return home by night, he would not marry her."

Paro's father went red as a beetroot. This was an insult he could not bear. His carefully built up reputation for honesty and decency was being rent apart now. What a struggle it had been for him to find a footing in this society, to earn a name that his children could feel proud to belong to! But how deceptively fragile this social status was. A gentle push could send him and his family teetering out of the reckoning of this society! He knew that he was on the brink of such a collapse now.

"Don't worry," he managed to choke out the words. "As soon as she is found, we will let you know." The assistant withdrew without another word.

Sarbari entered the scene. Debu's father looked quite frightening. His big eyes were bulging from their sockets. He was red-faced and his big moustache bristled with anger and emotion. Sarbari stammered out her message, almost in tears. She was, after all, a little girl.

Debu's mother shrieked when she heard that Debu had left in search of his little sister: "*Sarbonash!*" Now she had lost both her children, she cried.

Hariprasad was very terrifying to look at now. "Did he say where he was going?" he roared at Sarbari.

"N...no." she stammered back in a dry thin voice. "Y..e..s, he is going to the school at Sonapara to meet *mastermoshai!*"

"What?!!" the wrathful roar seemed to shake the whole house. Sarbari trembled and shook like a butterfly's wings in the rain. "I'll book that *mastermoshai* for kidnapping. I'll have him whipped. He has brainwashed this girl. He has ruined me. I'll not spare him...." And he turned his attention to Sarbari. "You, girl, you study in that school, don't you?"

Sarbari did not wait to reply. She turned tail and fled!

Debu's father turned to the door and began striding out. "Leave that girl alone," said his wife in a weak voice. "Poor child. Let her go in peace." She thought her husband was after Sarbari.

He turned his fierce glare on her. "That school was set up to ruin decent families like ours. It will breed wild and disobedient girls. I won't let that *mastermoshai* ruin my family. I'm going to the *thana* to book a case of kidnapping!" And off he went.

8

SONAPARA AT LAST

The three women surrounded Paromita. Their faces were almost covered by the *aanchal* of the sari over their heads. Their saris were blowing in the cool evening breeze all around them.

Paro could hardly see their faces—it had grown so dark by now. She could only vaguely make out the figures of the three women and she knew they too were studying her, taking in her crumpled and soiled sari, her muddy feet, her uncombed, unkempt hair—what did they think of her?

They looked at her with suspicion.

"Who are you, my child? How is it that you are going alone? Is there no one with you?" asked one of them, an elderly woman, in a gentle motherly tone. She was tall and towered over the little girl.

"Have you run away from home?" this was a younger woman, thin and fair, who looked her up and down mercilessly and then glared at her with disapproval.

Paro did not know what to say. She cast down her eyes and would not look up. "I've come to meet *mastermoshai* at Sonapara," she replied quite truthfully. "Yes, I've come alone from Gobindopur."

"But tomorrow is Sunday. No school," said the young woman, who was being quite unpleasant. "Why should you want to meet *mastermoshai*? Are you his student?"

"No, I'm not his student yet, said Paro."

"How did your parents allow you to go out alone?" asked the elderly woman, frowning. She seemed angrier with the parents than with Paro.

"She **must** have run away from home," the younger woman sounded quite definite.

Then the third woman came forward. She came close to Paro and peered closely at her. She was plump, cheerful-looking and short. "O *ma*! Look at her feet—they're bleeding. She has come from far. You must be very tired, my dear," she said and put her hand on Paro's dishevelled hair. Hearing the kind words, Paro, who was terribly exhausted, nearly broke down. But she controlled herself with grit and refused to meet their eyes.

The plump woman, whom the other two called Parboti, looked at her with compassion, while the younger one just behind her, muttered away under her breath.

"Well, never mind all that," Parboti dismissed the words of the disapproving man behind her. "It's dark and she needs rest. Let us take her to *mastermoshai's* house in Sonapara. Dipali *boudi* will take care of the rest. You can tell us your story tomorrow, *theek to?*" she asked caressing Paro's head.

"*Theek aachey, mashi ma.*" mumbled Paro, who was too tired to even speak. That settled the matter and the women continued on their way with Paro. Even the younger woman did not grumble any more. The plump woman, who had a sweet voice, took Paro's hand in hers and gently cajoled her on with words of encouragement.

It was night when they reached Sonapara. The glow of the firefly lit up their path as they passed the occasional cart that was returning to the village after a long journey. The birds had gone to roost and except for the occasional cuckoo that cooed sleepily, the song of the cricket, and the collective croaking of frogs in ditches, there was no other sound.

Paro was terribly hungry and tired and her knees buckled now and then.

At last, they reached *mastermoshai's* little house and knocked on the door. The door was opened by a young woman with a pleasant smiling face. The bright red vermilion that filled the parting of her hair shone in the dim light of the lantern she carried. When she saw the three women, she placed the lantern in a crevice in the wall, hurriedly draped the *aanchal* of her sari over her head and stepped aside to let them in. *"Aashun aashun, didi! Ki khobor? Eto ratre…?"* she asked, a little worried to see them at this unusual time.

"No, no, Dipali, nothing to worry," assured the elderly woman, entering the house. She was followed by her two companions, and Paro sandwiched between them.

"Boudi, we have brought you a young guest!" said the plump Parboti as she propelled Paro in front of her.

"This is Paromita from Gobindopur and she has come here to meet *mastermoshai"* announced the elderly woman.

"But he isn't here now…" Dipali *boudi* looked uncertainly at Paro, a little surprised. The younger woman took her aside and whispered something to her. *Boudi* was back in a jiffy and she took Paro's arm kindly.

"Mastermoshai has gone to the city, but he will be back tomorrow morning. You can wait for him here. Come, let us have dinner. You must be hungry and sleepy."

When Dipali *boudi* took gentle but firm control of the situation, the women left.

Paro looked around her and peered into the semi-darkness of the little one-roomed mud house. Biswajit and Dipali lived in simplicity. Two chairs, a table, some shelves full of books, some bedding rolled up and stuffed into a corner, some big wooden chests covered neatly with sheets—that was the sum total of their worldly belongings.

About fifteen steps away from the main door was a short wall that partitioned the kitchen from the rest of the house. *Boudi* disappeared into the kitchen, inviting Paro to join her. The girl followed her and sat down in a corner quietly watching *boudi* lay out the plates for dinner. "There's some *tarkari* and some *dalna* for dinner. Do you like *rui maach*? There's some of that too. Of course, it may not taste like your mother's food…but you must eat well. You look very, very tired."

The mention of her mother was just too much, but Paro fought back the tears that threatened to flood her. She had left her mother behind and she had not even thought about when she would see her again. When would she ever taste the *rui maach* that her mother fried specially for her? Or the *maacher jhol* at home that tasted better than that she had had in all other houses where she had eaten—her *thakurma's,* all her *pishis'*, her neighbours…nobody made it as well as her mother. Would she ever again nestle in her mother's warm lap and drop off to sleep and pleasant dreams? Could she hope to cuddle up to *ma* again when she took her afternoon siesta?

But Paro was a brave girl. "Look forward," she told herself and brushed off the tears that threatened. She had not thought of what she would do next. All she knew was that she must reach school and get admitted somehow and stop the marriage immediately. The marriage had to be stopped at any cost! It worried her that *mastermoshai* was not going to be home till tomorrow. If only no one came to catch her till he had returned and admitted her to his school. The rest of her life would take off from there.

Surely she could go back home after getting admitted to school. Surely her parents would welcome her with relief and love. After she began reading and writing, they would be proud of her. But her father did not understand the importance of all that to her. And so she had to work out a plan for her future.

A million thoughts and memories jostled in her young mind. Paro kept her emotions under a leash—perhaps better than most adults would, under the circumstances. She had reached her destination...the thought comforted her. She must study, she must wear spectacles and become a teacher, her parents would be proud of her, even her father...she dropped off to sleep, still thinking.

When the plates were laid, Dipali turned and found the girl huddled in a corner, fast asleep. "*Bechara!*" she whispered tenderly. She gently shook Paro awake and fed her. As she tucked her young guest into a makeshift bed, she wondered what the morrow would bring.

9

SUNDAY SCENES

Sunday dawned in Sonapara, bright and clear. The distant rumble of thunder attracted the attention of Dipali who was watering the plants in her little kitchen garden. She looked up. Patches of dark clouds were sailing across the sky.

"Will it rain?" she asked herself doubtfully as she surveyed the bright rosy sun rising on the horizon. It looked peaceful and serene...but one could never say.

And that little girl, sleeping so peacefully inside...who could she be? What could have brought her here all alone? She wanted to see *mastermoshai*. But she was not one of his students, Dipali was sure about that.

She knew all his students, because she attended school too! She was the oldest in the class, but she did not mind that. She thanked god for giving her such a generous and liberal husband, who wanted her to learn all that she had not learnt as a child. "In a few months from now, you must be able to independently handle classes and I shall turn my attention to recruiting more girls to our school from the villages around us," her husband had told her, just after the school was inaugurated six and half months back. She respected the target he had set and worked diligently to meet it.

"*Boudi!*" a voice startled her out of her reverie. She looked towards the gate. A scruffy young lad was standing there. He looked bedraggled and dirty, as if he had not slept but walked the streets the whole night.

"*Boudi!*" he said again. "Is this *mastermoshai's* house?"

"Yes" she replied, wondering who he was. Another child, now! Where were these children coming from?

"Can I see *mastermoshai!*" he sounded quite desperate.

"He is not home. He has gone to the city and should be back anytime now... who are you?"

The boy was frantically looking all around, as if he was searching for something. Dipali sighed and put down the vessel of water: an unknown girl sleeping inside the house, and a strange boy standing at her gate! What more was in store for her this day? Why wasn't her husband here yet?

"*Ke go tumi?* Who are you? Why do you want to meet my husband?" she asked.

"I'm...I'm...have you seen my younger sister? I think she must have come here looking for *mastermoshai!*"

Boudi stared. "Is your sister's name Paromita?"

"Yes, yes!" a radiant smile lit up the boy's face. "Is she here?"

"She's sleeping inside! Come in," said Dipali.

And the day is just beginning, she thought wryly, as she ushered the boy in. The city bus must have arrived. Her husband must be on his way home.

"Paro, O Paro!" Debu ran to his sister in joy and relief and shook her awake. And was Paro thrilled to see her darling *dada!*

"Why did you run away? Do you know how worried we all were? And your marriage tomorrow! Baba is furious! What happened?" the questions tumbled out.

Paro pushed Debu away suddenly. A doubt had crept into her mind. With narrowing eyes and knitted brows, she asked him "How did you find me? Are you going to take me back there? I won't come. I must meet *mastermoshai. I* won't marry. No matter what happens." She pushed back the hair that fell across her eyes and looked at him stubbornly. "Go back, *dada.* I won't come with you. And if you tell them I'm here, I won't speak to you ever again."

Dipali quietly watched, trying to piece together the disjointed information and make sense of it.

"*Ogo, shuncho!*" called a voice from the gate and Dipali turned to the door with relief. Her husband was back.

Biswajit entered his house but stopped in surprise at the threshold. Who were these two children? Had he not seen that girl before? Those eyes...!

Dipali went forward to relieve him of the bags he was carrying. "These two children are from Gobindopur! They need some help. They've been anxious to meet you."

Biswajit pulled up a chair and sat down. "Haven't I seen you at Gobindopur...near *Kalibari*?"

"*Han, mastermoshai*" answered Paromita, her eyes shining. So he remembered her. Surely he would help her! She shivered with excitement.

The two adults in the room were looking uncertainly at their young uninvited guests.

It was Paro who began. "*Mastermoshai,* let me stay here. I'll help *boudi* at home and come to school with you." *Mastermoshai* looked at her silently.

"I'll pay her school fees. I'll work somewhere and earn for her fees!" The boy burst out. Biswajit turned to him, still silent.

"I won't get married." That was Paromita again.

"It's not fair. They can't force her." That was Debu.

"I won't become a *sati*." said Paro.

Biswajit's eyes opened wide. O god! What were these children saying?

"Wait, wait, wait! Now what is all this about? How do you expect me to help you if you don't tell me your whole story?" he asked. Between them Paro and Debu narrated all that had happened.

"Tomorrow is your marriage and you have run away from home?" Biswajit's eyes opened wide in horror. "What shame are you bringing on your parents?"

"But how can such a little girl be married—specially against her will and to such an old man?" murmured Dipali, softly firm.

"I don't want to marry. I want to study," Paro's brows were still knitted. There was fire in her eyes.

"I think we must talk to your father about this," said Biswajit.

"I've told you, *mastermoshai*" she shook her head impatiently. "It's no use. *Baba* will not send me to school."

"But why?" asked Biswajit.

"He believes that girls must be married and boys must go to school," said Debu.

"Both boys and girls must be married, but not at *your* age. At your age, both girls and boys must study equally," Dipali's voice was soft and steady, and the smile had not left her face.

"That's all very well, Dipali," said Biswajit brusquely. "But do you realise that we have a problem here? This girl's parents must be searching for her. And you know our society. They do not look kindly on girls who have disappeared for a day or two, and that too, just before her marriage. The girls' marriage will break up. And in the future, who will marry her? And because she is here, we are party to this too. We can't do anything without her father's consent, do you realise that?"

"But I don't want to marry. I'm happy the marriage will break." Paro spoke in right earnest.

Biswajit sighed. "You're a child. You won't understand."

"That's what father always says. But he is wrong! I know what I want!" answered Paro. She was quite desperate. She had pinned high hopes on this *mastermoshai* but he was so hesitant to help. Dipali *boudi* was more understanding. Perhaps she might convince him... Paro turned to her impulsively with a pleading look.

"The damage has been done by this child running away. Now we must plan for her future. Now, more than ever, she needs the support of education," Dipali *boudi* argued, in response to Paro's mute appeal.

"If you won't let me study, I'll go away somewhere, I don't know where. But I'll not go back home and I won't marry!" Paro's eyes flashed with anger.

She's looking just like *baba* now, thought Debu. He knew his father would skin him if he knew what was going on here. But Paro needed help and support now. However Debu was too mild and timid to know what to do next.

Paro was not finished with Biswajit. "This is a school for girls, isn't it? Then how can you deny me permission to study? You're a teacher. Should you not convince girls to attend school? And when I come seeking a place in your school, you want to send me back?" She did not blink at all as her eyes blazed with fury at *mastermoshai*.

Biswajit chewed his lower lip thoughtfully. He knew she was right. His wife was right, too. But this was a tricky situation.

Before he could say anything, the gate creaked open. "This is the house," came a loud, furious voice. "Call him out!" said somebody else. "*Mastermoshai, O, mastermoshai!*"

10

PARO'S FUTURE

The door swung open and in walked an odd threesome. There was a policeman in the lead, then a villager and then—Paro's father, twirling his walking stick furiously in his hand.

The policeman looked distinctly uncomfortable. Behind his ferocious moustache, the stiff khaki shirt and shorts and the cane in his hand, he was a man of peace. He did not like emotional scenes and he knew that he was on the verge of one. He had groaned when he had agreed to follow the landlord, Hariprasad of Gobindopur. These landlords were all the same, they behaved as if everyone they encountered worked for them—for a pittance of a salary, of course.

He saw the group in the house, looking at them. The little girl with the big eyes, the thoughtful man, the woman with her face partially covered by the *aanchal* over the head, and the young boy with tousled hair. They did not know what was coming. Or did they?

The villager was quivering like a leaf in a storm. He did not want anything to do with a *daroga* and a strange angry landlord. He had been picked out to show them the way to *mastermoshai's* house, and that was bad enough.

"Th..that..at's *mastermoshai*" he managed to rasp out.

"Thank you for your help, my man. I can manage henceforth," and Hariprasad Choudhry said, turning to him very abruptly and fixing him with a stony glare. The man took the hint and thankfully bolted out of the house.

"*Daroga babu*, arrest him!" ordered Hariprasad, pointing his walking stick at Biswajit. "He has kidnapped my children." There he goes, thought the *daroga*, just as I expected. A real life *jatra*!

"Kidnapped!" Dipali was the first to react. "He returned from Kolkata only ten minutes ago. These children have come here by themselves."

"Don't interfere, woman," Hariprasad retorted. "What are you waiting for, *darogar*! Let us take him to the *thana*"

Biswajit stood up from the chair. "But Hariprasad *babu*, I don't have a warrant..." But the *daroga's* feeble voice was cut short by the raging Hariprasad. "Did you not say you would take back the culprits to the police *thana*? I have booked a complaint against him. Now will you do your duty?"

As the *daroga* moved towards Biswajit uncertainly, Paro screamed out, 'Don't arrest *mastermoshai*. He has not brought us here…"

"Shut up," barked her father. "Carry on, *daroga*. You want to listen to minor children like that? He has brainwashed them."

'*Na, darogababu, na*," Debu jumped forward to take hold of the policeman's hand. The walking stick swung in the air. Debu tried to grab it but failed. It landed with a crackling sound on Debu's back. The sting and the shock immobilised him. Paro rushed to him with a scream and Dipali covered her face with a shudder. She couldn't bear violence. Biswajit walked forward angrily. "Enough of this violence, *moshai*. You want me to go to the *thana*. I'll come. But don't hit the children. Come let's go!"

Hariprasad grabbed Paro's hand roughly. "Come! You've done enough mischief. Now we must seek Manik *babu's* pardon."

"No, never! I won't go home!" Paro screamed all the way to her father's carriage.

It was a strange group that walked out of Biswajit's hut that morning. Hariprasad marched out first, still red with anger, Paro's tender wrist in his iron grasp. Debu followed, still rubbing his back, tired and hungry after his sleepless night under the skies on the road. Behind them, the *daroga*, thankful that the show had ended quickly, escorted Biswajit out. Dipali watched helplessly.

While Hariprasad and his children got into his horse-drawn carriage, Biswajit and the *daroga* got into the policeman's cycle. The silent procession made its way to the police station in the town of Ramnagar, near Gobindopur.

11

ENTER THE POLICE

Late last night, when Hariprasad had marched into the *thana* to lodge a complaint against the school teacher, Inspector Jones had not been there. The *daroga* on duty had advised him to come early in the morning. Hariprasad had returned home, frustrated by his helplessness.

He strode around the house like a hungry lion all night, debating whether he should surprise Biswajit by barging into the school at Sonapara at night. But his hysterical mother had fallen in a faint and the doctor had been summoned. His weeping sister and wife could not be trusted to take charge of the house in his absence. He instinctively realised that Sarbari must be right and Paro must be at school in the master's custody.

Paro's marriage was as good as finished and he boiled at the thought. What effort had gone through to contract the marriage with the richest and most distinguished bachelor in the village! Hariprasad had no doubts about the suitability of the groom—never mind the age, he did not consider it a factor in marriage. And the foolish girl had not only ruined her own life but made him look a fool in the village.

The next morning, even before his wife had boiled the milk for his first cup of *cha*, Hariprasad had been out of the house. His driver was commanded to appear **at once** and the poor man came running from the other end of the village. One more trip to the Ramnagar police station— because Paro's father was keen on seeing that the obnoxious schoolteacher who spoiled the minds of girls, be arrested and punished.

But once again, the Inspector was not there. "The *gora sahebs* don't come so early," the *daroga* on duty had explained. But Hariprasad's patience was wearing thin. "Do you want me to wait for your inspector—my children may be butchered by their kidnappers by then—will you take the responsibility for that?" he snapped at the *daroga*, fixing him with his fiery eyes. And the man was trapped.

He told the landlord to write out his complaint, and then took up his headgear and *lathi*. Leaving the *thana* in the charge of the guard on duty, he followed the angry landlord out. "Let us go and see, *moshai*, and bring the culprits back here," he had said and Hariprasad had agreed.

And so the *daroga,* grumbling to himself that his day had started on a sad note, and the bristling landlord had rolled down the rickety road that led to Sonapara. They crossed the *pukka* bridge across the river that all vehicles took and reached the village.

Now they took the same route back to the Ramnagar police station. By the time they reached their destination, the sun was up and blazing and all of them were perspiring freely. There was no sign of that rumbling thunder that Dipali had heard with misgiving that morning.

The *thana* that was dark and damp last night, looked bright and smart in the morning. The guards on duty did not slouch now: they stood smartly at attention, guns down. The chairs and tables and the low wooden benches had been dusted clean. All because Inspector Jones had arrived promptly, after attending church service that Sunday morning.

Passersby stared as the horse-drawn carriage drew up at the police station and the tall, straight figure of the landlord and his two tired children got off and walked in. The *thana* was actually an embarrassment to the town. The people who lived in that street liked to pretend it did not exist. The only people who entered it were criminals and poor people whom the British called criminals. And of course, some occasional rebels, who spoke against the British, were punished heavily too.

Tall and tanned deep brown in the Bengal sunshine, Inspector Jones' word was law in the district. He had never been known to smile and his voice was always cold. But he was known to be fair and just to everyone: Englishmen and natives alike. He shot one look at Hariprasad from under his bushy brown eyebrows and gestured to him and Biswajit to sit in front of him.

"Yes?" he rasped crisply. Hariprasad, in a mixture of bad English and simple *Bangla,* tried to explain what had happened. Like most other Englishmen who came to India and dealt everyday with Indians, Inspector Jones too, not only knew Bangla, he also spoke it reasonably well. He heard Hariprasad out with growing impatience and when his voice had tapered off, he looked keenly around at the other players in the drama. He saw the young dishevelled girl with bright eyes, the unkempt boy with the sullen look and tousled hair, Biswajit with a resigned face and the *darogar,* looking helpless and nervous.

It took Inspector Jones just ten minutes to understand that Hariprasad actually had no case at all. "I have more important things to do!" he told Hariprasad firmly. "Take your family rows elsewhere."

"He kidnapped my daughter!" Hariprasad bridled with indignation at being dismissed like that.

"I've known Biswajit for many years now," said the Inspector, not concealing his impatience. "He is an associate of Pandit Ishwarchandra Vidyasagar. He is a city-bred boy who has come all the way to Sonapara to carry forward Vidyasagar *moshai's* campaign for girls' education. So kindly stop imagining things. He is no kidnapper."

"He has brainwashed my daughter. He and the school will ruin our society. Our society forbids girls from going to school. But this man and his friends are breaking our social rules. He is giving girls crazy ideas. He has made my daughter run away from home to him."

"Now you say your daughter ran away. Just five minutes ago you said Biswajit had kidnapped her. What do you mean? Don't contradict yourself."

Hariprasad stuttered and stammered and lapsed into sullen silence.

"Here, let us ask your daughter what happened. *Aeije, meye,* come here."

Paro came forward, eyes downcast, not daring to look either at the Inspector or her father. "Now did you run away or did he kidnap you?"

"I ran away. *Mastermoshai* did not do anything."

"Why did you run away?"

"Because I did not want to get married. My marriage is fixed for tomorrow!"

The inspector's eyes narrowed as he turned his cold glare at Hariprasad. 'You didn't say anything about marriage! You want this child married?...How old are you, you girl?"

"Nine and a half."

The inspector turned to Hariprasad. "And who is to be her bridegroom?"

Hariprasad did not dare face him now. "Manik *babu,* the big *zamindar* of Gobindopur!".

There was a silence. "That man is older than you! How do you have the heart to get this beautiful little girl married to an old man like that?"

Now it was Hariprasaad's turn to keep quiet. Paro looked at her father. Never had anyone spoken to him like that. She had always thought no one could dream of defying her father—except she, that is!

"Are you a father or a monster?"

"Don't insult me, Inspector. I'm doing my best for my children. You don't understand..." Hariprasad struggled to his feet, frustrated and stuttering.

"He is not a monster!" shouted Paro, indignant with the inspector. "He wants to do me good, but he does not know what is good for me! But don't call him a monster!"

She was hurt and shocked to see her confident father stuttering and stammering. Nobody spoke like that to him. Everyone stood up respectfully when father entered the room. And here was this inspector who had reduced that strong man to speechlessness. How dare he?

"Shut up, Haribabu and you, girl, let me speak!" Inspector Jones' voice was like ice. "It is stupid to marry off a girl at the age of nine. If your daughter wants to go to school, kindly send her. She seems to have more sense than you do!"

Hariprasad was furious, of course. But he was quite helpless too. He could not book Biswajit under the law— his agenda had been defeated. Hariprasad did not know how to cope with defeat. He had never been defeated before. He turned and marched out of the police station, mortified. He got into his carriage and sat quietly. The children ran behind him and Biswajit followed uncertainly, not knowing what to do.

Paro hopped into the carriage and took her father's hand hesitantly. *"Baba,* shall we go home?" Her father would not say a word. *"Dada,* get in!" Debu got in quietly.

"Mastermoshai, please forgive me for all the trouble I've caused you and *boudi"* Paro whispered from the carriage, hands folded.

Biswajit looked at her, tongue-tied. Was this girl giving up her battle? The carriage started off. He stood looking at it disappearing fast down the road, raising clouds of dust. And dust was what he felt in his dry mouth.

12

THE TURNAROUND

Paro's face danced before Biswajit's eyes all the way back to Sonapara. And he could not quite face his wife as he recounted what had happened at the *thana*. "And you kept quiet and let all that happen?" she asked in a small voice.

"Dipali, o Dipali," called a voice from outside. Dipali peeped out of the house. It was the plump and cheerful Parboti. She had seen *mastermoshai* walk up to his house just two minutes ago and she wanted to know what was being done to Paromita.

"Your *swami* is back?" she asked.

"Yes, *didi!*" said Dipali.

"What about that girl, Paro? Has your husband found out what the matter was?"

"Yes, *didi*. Paro has gone back to her house with her father."

"I knew it. Whatever the problem, your husband will solve it. He is a wise man." And happy in the thought that Paro had been returned safely to her house, Parboti walked away. She could come back to Dipali for details when Biswajit was not around.

Biswajit had heard Parboti. He looked up at Dipali. Her eyes showed her utter disappointment and dejection. "Everyone believes in you. That inspector called you Vidyasagar *moshai's* associate!" she said and turned away with that. But how those words stung him!

Back in Gobindopur, when the carriage entered the village, there was excitement everywhere. News travelled very fast. Everyone peeped out of windows and doors to see the carriage and the silent threesome in it. Sarbari blinked back tears of joy when she heard the news. She had seen the messenger from Manik *babu's* house the last evening and when she had recounted the story at home, her mother had commented that Paro's marriage was as good as finished. It did not matter. At least, she was back and safe. Maybe she would again join her friends in their games in the fields and groves.

The carriage came to a stop in front of Hariprasad's house. There was a flurry of excitement next door. Out of the corner of her eye, Paro could see Chitra *boudi's* billowing sari disappearing into the house. "So even she has heard that I'm back," thought Paro as she alighted from the carriage and followed her father in.

Her mother had rushed to the door and hugged the girl tightly without a word. Tears coursed down her cheeks and as she caressed her. "How could you leave me and go away?" she murmured in a broken voice.

"Give that girl a bath!" crackled Hariprasad. His wife loosened her grip. "I'll get some hot water ready. Debu, *paagal chhele,* why did you disappear like that? You love your sister so much, do you?" And much to his embarrassment, *ma* took Debu's face in her hands and planted a kiss on his smooth forehead.

Mejo pishi and *thakurma* and an assortment of relatives walked in and out of the room, muttering and whispering to each other, but not daring to talk aloud in the face to Hariprasad's curtness.

Soon there was complete silence in Hariprasad's house. No one quite knew what to say or do. The joy of seeing Paro back home had evaporated at the sight of Hariprasad's stony face.

As he entered the room, he tore down the festoons lining the doorway of the *puja* room with a vicious movement of his stick. The women in the house were petrified. The noisy clatter of vessels in the kitchen and the *pandal* outside had died after the visit of Manik *babu's* messenger.

Now after the return of the would-be bride, the house looked even more gloomy and grim. Everyone sat around unsurely, as if waiting for something to happen. Paro and Debu were quiet and hushed.

After a couple of hours of terrible silence, *mejo pishi* decided to cheer everyone up. She brought out those gleaming bangles as the family sat to dinner. "Look, Paro, these are for you. Do you like them?"

Pat came Paro's reply: "*Mejo pishi*, they are beautiful. But there's no marriage happening here. You better go home tomorrow!" And she sneaked a sidelong look at her father. *Mejo pishi's* jaw dropped! But Hariprasad maintained his stony silence.

That night, Hariprasad had a guest. It was Biswajit. Hariprasad met him with an icy look.

"I've come to you with a petition, Haribabu," began Biswajit. "God has blessed you with an intelligent daughter. A girl with a firm and steady character, one who knows her mind. It is you duty to encourage her. Not only your duty, sir, but mine too. I'm ashamed that I've failed in my duty. I should have recognised her promise when I first met her and I should've tried to convince you...we could have avoided all these sad incidents, had I done that...but it's still not too late..."

Hariprasad led him into a room and shut the door behind them. He sat in cold silence. His face was blank, his eyes did not blink and his unflinching gaze did not leave Biswajit's face. He let him talk on, for which Biswajit was quite grateful although he did not know whether the man even heard a word. After half an hour, Hariprasad broke in with a question...

For two hours, the men were closeted.

Paro and Debu wondered what was going on. So did their mother. "Do you think he will send me to school?" asked Paro, her interest reviving at the sight of Biswajit. Debu shook his head: "*Baba*? Will he change his mind? I don't think so."

"But why do you think *mastermoshai* is here?" asked Paro, quite logically.

"Maybe to apologise for what has happened," replied Debu.

"But he didn't do anything wrong!" cried Paro.

"Do you think *baba* will force him to close the school and go away from Sonapara?" asked Debu.

"Oh no!" Paro was quite horrified.

"You know how powerful *baba* is. When he wants something, he will do it!" said Debu.

"Yes," said Paro. But she remembered the scene at the police station, and was not quite convinced.

"Move, children, if *baba* comes out suddenly and finds you here, he will be angry with you" said mother but she just could not push the children away from the door. "*Na, ma*, my life depends on this," said Paro.

Then they heard the handle on the door turn and they jumped away from it—in time. The door opened and revealed a grim-faced Hariprasad. "Paro, come in," he said and disappeared into the room once again. Paro walked in immediately, her heart thudding suddenly...painfully.

Mrinalini, who was sitting with Swarnalata a little away, got up and came running to the door, as it swung shut on her face. Debu, looking ashen, stood at the door and she joined him. "*Kee hobe?*" she whispered, half in terror. They stared at the shut door and listened keenly to try and listen to the conversation.

Two minutes seemed like two hours for Mrinalini and Debu. Then they heard some loud screams and shouts of "*Baba!*" This was just too much for them. Mrinalini, fearing for her daughter's very life, pushed open the door and flew into the room followed by Debu.

They saw Paro in her father's arms, hugging him tightly and squealing. "*Baba*, honestly? Do you mean it?"

They stopped in their tracks, surprised. "*Ma, dada*, I'm going to school from tomorrow," Paro announced, smiling through her tears. "*Baba* has agreed to send me to school."

Hariprasad had listened to all that Biswajit had to say. He had known that the marriage was now just not possible. But what would happen to a girl whose marriage broke off because she had run away? Yes, indeed, Hariprasad knew in his heart of hearts that Inspector Jones was quite right. His prospective son-in-law was older than he was. Of course, where social standing and prospects were concerned, Paro could not have made a better match. But her personal relations with the old man might have been

difficult…but all that was the past. Should he agree to send her to school now? What a comedown that would be for him! He could not face anyone in the village after that.

As Biswajit spoke on and on, he realised that he could not destroy the girl's dreams and aspirations, just for the sake of appearing like a mightly decision-maker to everyone. It was only because he had stuck to his opinion and refused to yield to her pleas for education that things had come to such a pass. He could not make things worse for her, for himself, for his silent wife, and his son, He made up his mind.

He opened the door and called Paro in. "Paro, you may go to school from tomorrow!" said her father stiffly. Paro stood, unbelieving! And in a trice, she was in his arms, hugging him with squeals of delight and joy. Hariprasad smiled and held her close. "Yes, *mastermoshai* is right. It is my duty to educate this wonderful girl. She will make me proud of her!" he thought, the ice broken. How swiftly the girl had pardoned him for all the anxious and trying days that he had given her. Waves of compassion swept the man's breast.

Then the spring came back to Paro's steps, and the dimples returned to her tender cheeks. But those eyes, they were different…not twinkling with mischief anymore, but glowing with confidence and the light of knowledge.

GLOSSARY

Aanchal: the mantle of the sari, that falls on the shoulder and streams down the back.

Aashun, aashun, mejdi: aashun means welcome and mejdi is middle sister

Acchha, baba: o.k. father

Alta: a red liquid, which is distilled from flowers and applied on their feet by girls.

Amar lokkhi meyeti: amar is my, lokkhi is good (the Bengali way of saying Lakshmi, the goddess of wealth) and meye-ti is girl

Ba, ki sundar: an exclamation of appreciation, oh, how beautiful!

Baba: father

Baccha meye to: little girl after all! Meye is girl.

Badmaish meye: naughty girl

Badmaish: mischievous

Baur: bridegroom

Bechara!: poor thing!

Boudi: brother's wife. Young married women are often called *boudi* in Bengal.

Bidai: the formal farewell of a bride from her maternal home.

Cha: tea

Chandan: sandal paste

Chiku: round, brown small sweet fruits, also known as sapota.

Da: short for dada or elder brother

Dadu: maternal grandfather

Dalna: vegetable dish.

Daroga: policeman

Dooshtu: mischievous

Durga: the manifestation of the Mother Goddess or Shakti, who is popularly worshipped in Bengal during the Durga Puja. She is believed to have killed the evil Mahishasura and established the triumph of right over might.

Eto rattire…?: so late at night?

Gora sahibs: white masters

Han: Yes

Jaba phool: hibiscus flower.

Jatra: a kind of folk theatre popular in Bengal. It is known for its drama, music, dance and loud dialogues.

Kalibari: means Kali's house. Temples of goddess Kali are called Kalibari.

Ke go tumi: who are you, my dear? 'Go' is a colloquial term used to address people with familiarity.

Kee hobe?: what will happen?

Ki kando!: an exclamation: what an incident! How shocking!

Ki khobor?: what news?

Koi, na to: koi is why and na to is no. A colloquial way of saying, 'why, no!'

Lathi: the baton or stick wielded by policemen.

Ma go: mother dear, an exclamation of surprise and sometimes of fear.

Maacher jhol: a dish made of fish

Mamoney: darling, a term of endearment

Mashi: mother's sister. Elderly women are respectfully called mashima in Bengal.

Mastermoshai: schoolteacher.

Mejo pishi: mejo middle and usually refers to the second of three brothers or sisters. *Pishi* is aunt, the sister of one's father. *Mejo pishi* means the second of three aunts.

Moshai: a term of respect that is used whilie addressing men

Moyra: a person who makes sweets.

Ogo, shunchhho: my dear, are you listening? A popular term of address between husband and wife.

Paagal chhele: mad boy

Paan: the betel leaves, of which there are several varieties in Bengal.

Pandal: a shamiana

Payesh: a sweet dish made of boiled and thickened milk with rice

Pola: bangle made of red lac worn by married women in Bengal

Punjabi: the kurta was adapted from the north Indian dress by the Bengali men.

Purohit: priest

Raja: king.

Rui maach: rohu, a kind of fish. Bengalis are enthusiastic fish-eaters!

Sarbonash: exclamation again: all is lost!

Sasurima: mother-in-law

Shankha: bangle made of conch shell, symbol of a woman's marital status in Bengal.

Shonamoney: shona is golden, so this means goldeh darling
Sindoor: sacred vermilion that married women fill in the parting
    of their hair. It is a symbol of the marital status of women.
Swami: husband
Tarkari: vegetable dish
Thakur's puja: thakur is god and puja is worship
Thakurma: paternal grandmother
Thakurpukur: literally means god's pond
Thana: police station
Theek aachhey: it is ok.
Theek to?: ok, isn't it?

Rupa /5/12/02